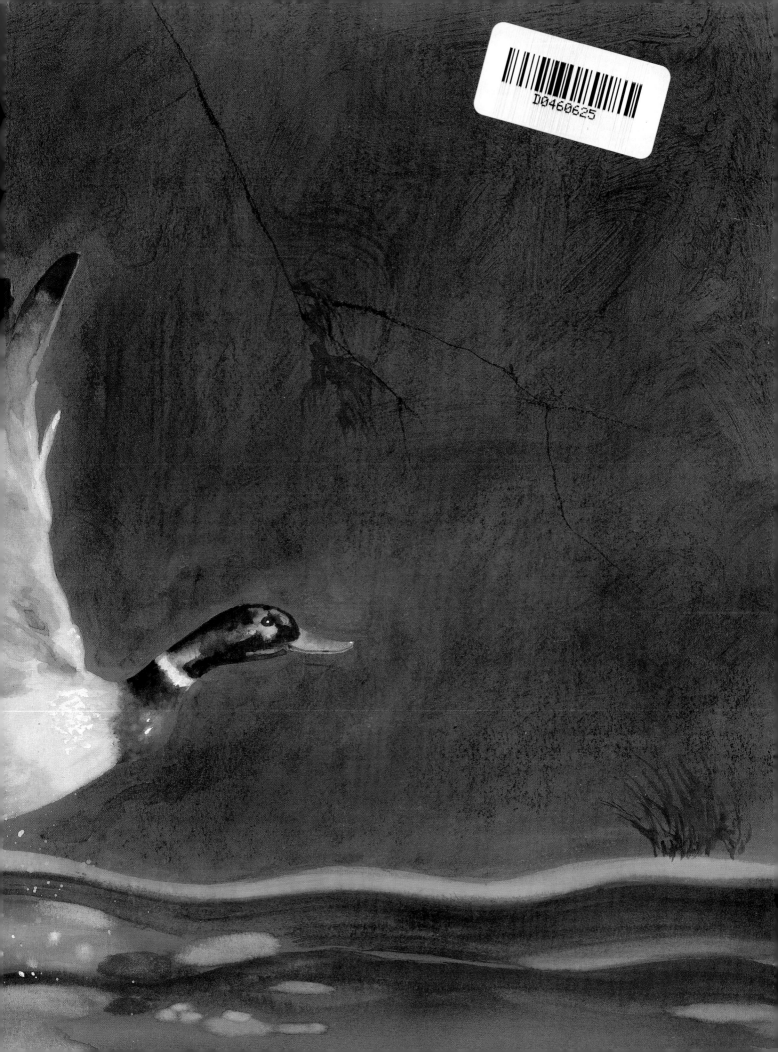

SECRET PLACE

SECRET PLACE

by EVE BUNTING
Illustrated by TED RAND

CLARION BOOKS/*New York*

Clarion Books
a Houghton Mifflin Company imprint
215 Park Avenue South, New York, NY 10003
Text copyright © 1996 by Edward D. Bunting and Anne E. Bunting Family Trust
Illustrations copyright © 1996 by Ted Rand

The illustrations for this book were executed in
transparent watercolor and pastel on 100% rag paper.
The text is set in 18/20-point Sabon.

www.clarionbooks.com

Printed in Singapore

Library of Congress Cataloging-in-Publication Data
Bunting, Eve, 1928–
Secret place / by Eve Bunting ; illustrated by Ted Rand.
p. cm.
Summary: A young boy finds a patch of wilderness in the city.
ISBN 0-395-64367-8
[1. City and town life—Fiction. 2. Nature—Fiction.]
I. Rand, Ted, ill.   II. Title
PZ7.B91527Se   1996
[E]—dc20   95-20466
CIP

ISBN-13: 978-0-395-64367-9
ISBN-10: 0-395-64367-8

TWP   20   19   18   17   16   15   14   13   12   11

To Ted Rand, with admiration and affection

E.B.

To Christopher Wells, 1984–1995

T.R.

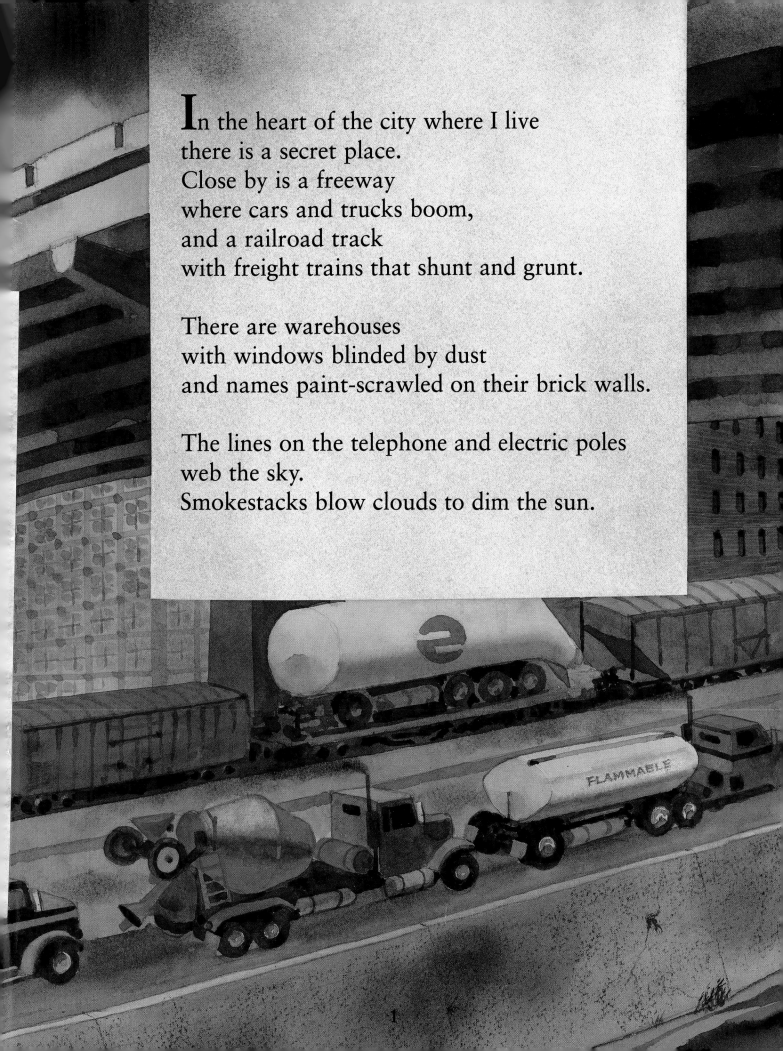

In the heart of the city where I live
there is a secret place.
Close by is a freeway
where cars and trucks boom,
and a railroad track
with freight trains that shunt and grunt.

There are warehouses
with windows blinded by dust
and names paint-scrawled on their brick walls.

The lines on the telephone and electric poles
web the sky.
Smokestacks blow clouds to dim the sun.

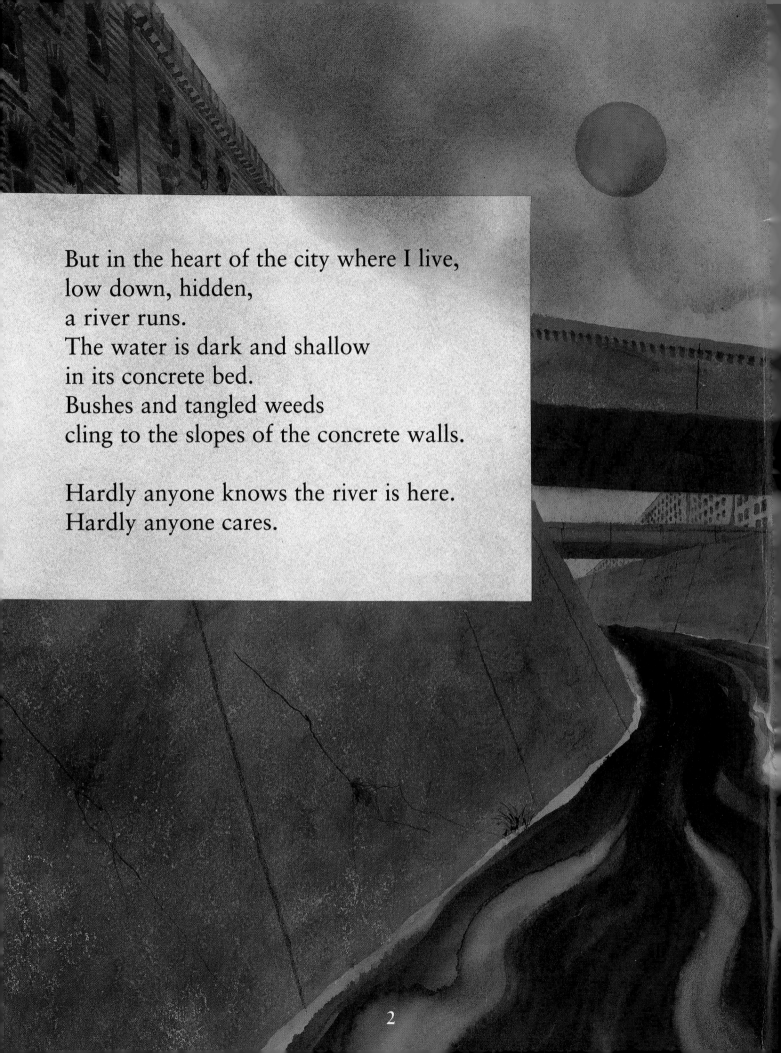

But in the heart of the city where I live,
low down, hidden,
a river runs.
The water is dark and shallow
in its concrete bed.
Bushes and tangled weeds
cling to the slopes of the concrete walls.

Hardly anyone knows the river is here.
Hardly anyone cares.

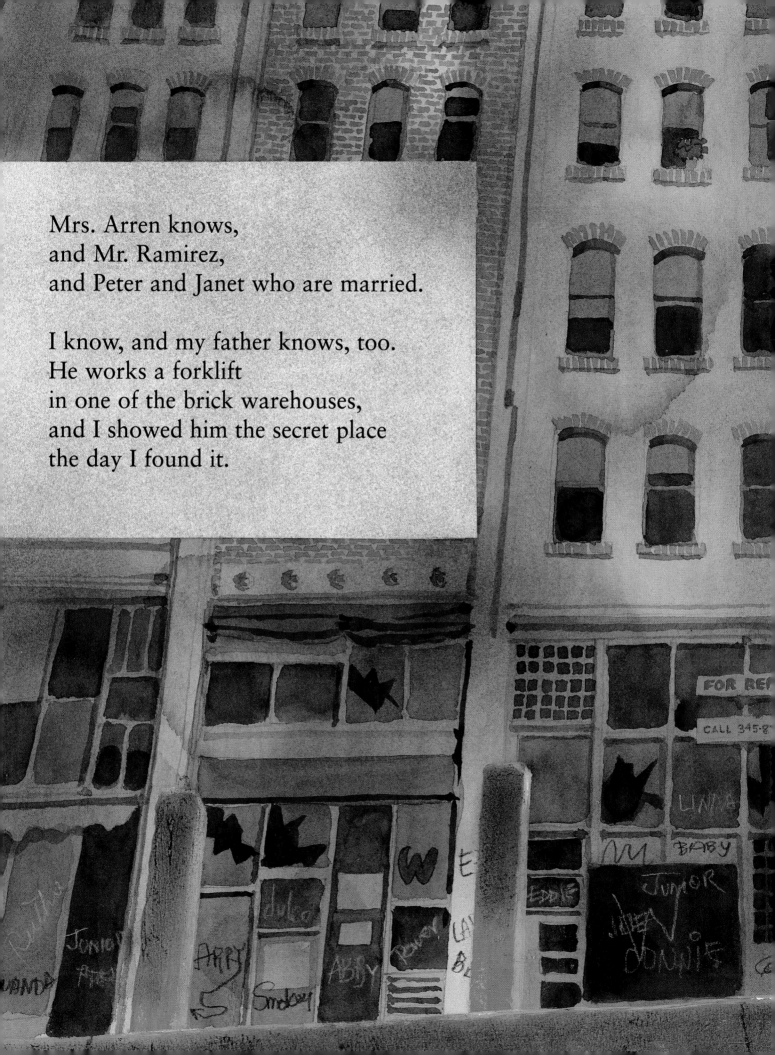

Mrs. Arren knows,
and Mr. Ramirez,
and Peter and Janet who are married.

I know, and my father knows, too.
He works a forklift
in one of the brick warehouses,
and I showed him the secret place
the day I found it.

The white egret found it, too.
I watch the bird float down,
its legs thin and reaching,
its head plumes fanned.

The green-winged teal knows.
The buffleheads that come to water-skim know.
And the circling mallards know.
I've seen them here before.
Peter says last year
there was a mallard nest
lined with feathers from the mother's breast.
Later there were ducklings.
"They'll nest here again," Peter says.
I jump up and down. "Ducklings! Perfect!"

sparrows

mallard.

bufflehead

coot

cinnamon teal

green-winged teal

Mrs. Arren and Mr. Ramirez and Janet and Peter
bring binoculars.
They let me look through them.
The sparrows lined up on the barbed wire fence
seem big as mud hens.

Peter tells me the names of the birds.
He is like a bird himself,
with hair the color of a cinnamon teal.

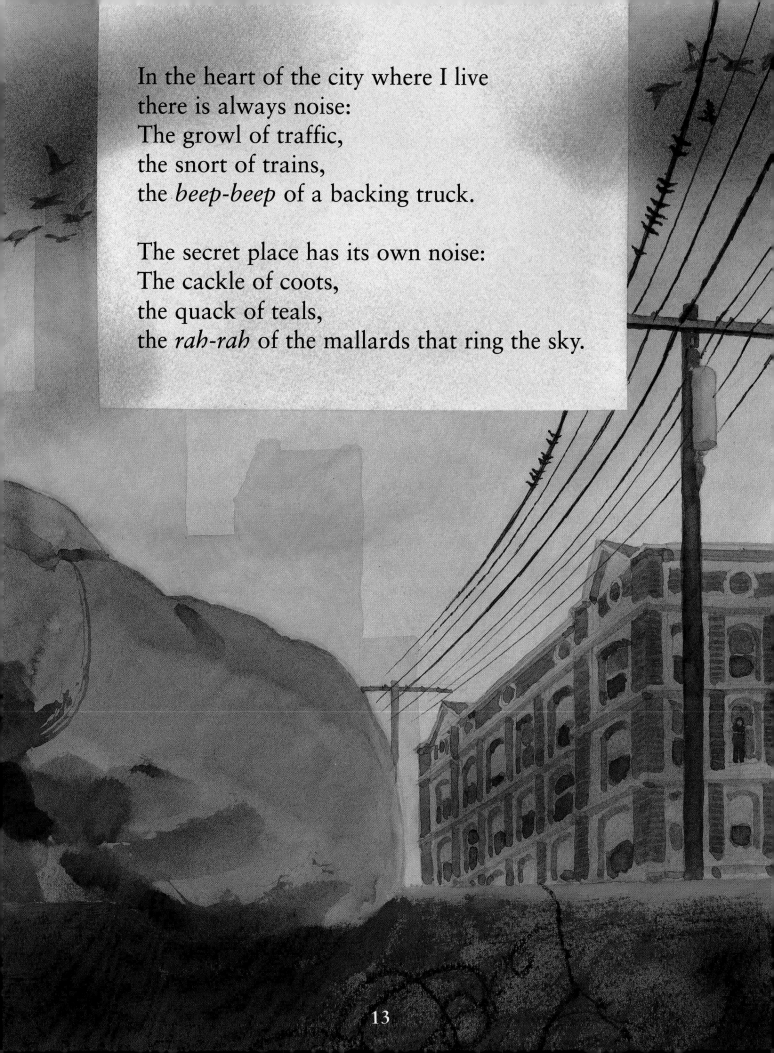

In the heart of the city where I live
there is always noise:
The growl of traffic,
the snort of trains,
the *beep-beep* of a backing truck.

The secret place has its own noise:
The cackle of coots,
the quack of teals,
the *rah-rah* of the mallards that ring the sky.

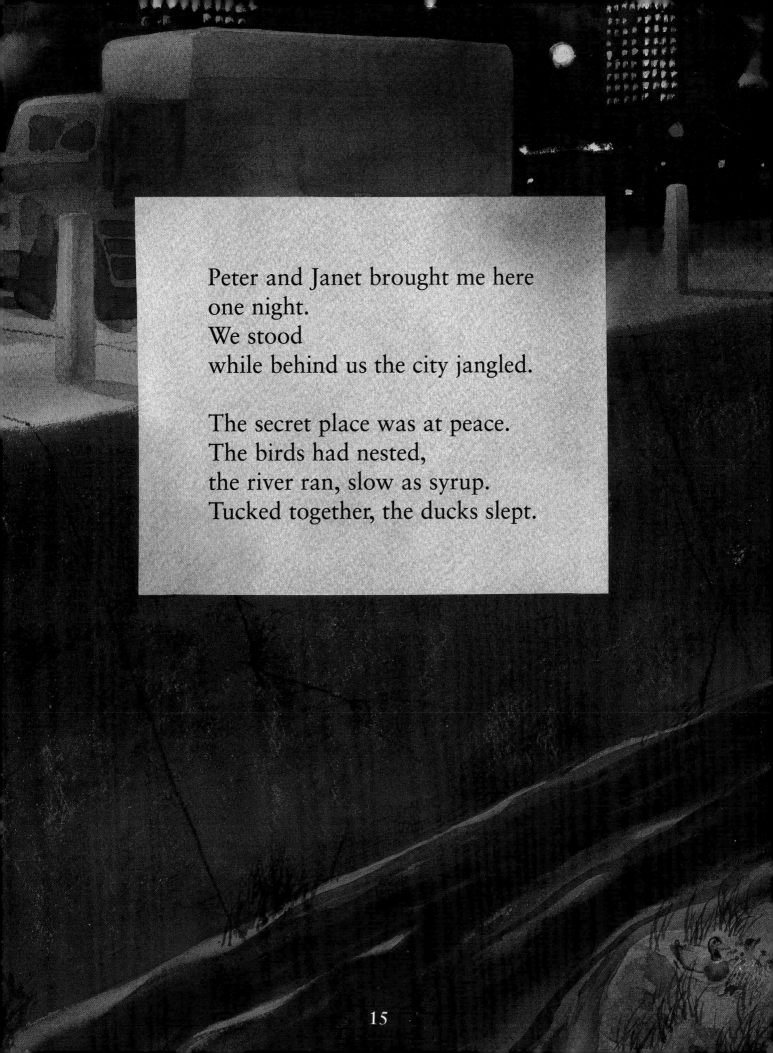

Peter and Janet brought me here
one night.
We stood
while behind us the city jangled.

The secret place was at peace.
The birds had nested,
the river ran, slow as syrup.
Tucked together, the ducks slept.

A coyote came
to lap the shadowed water.
A possum
carried her children to drink.

"How did they find this place?" I asked.
"They have always been here," Janet said.
"Before the city grew
there was wilderness.
This is all that's left.
Wild things need quiet.
We do, too."

20

The phone wires rocked the moon
in their cradle of lines.
The stars rested bright on the telephone poles.

"I want to tell everyone
what's here," I said.
"Be careful," Peter said.
"Some people might want
to take the secret place
and change it."

"I'd never want that to happen," I said.
"I told my father,
but he is good with secrets.
I will be careful who else I tell."

I will only say that
close to a freeway
and a railroad track
and tall smoking chimneys,
in the heart of the city where I live
there is a secret place.

If you can find it,
there may be ducklings.